My Cat Isis

To cat and goddess lovers everywhere,
and to Geoff, Sawyer and Daimon, who all
claim to have named our cat Isis — C.A.

To my two cats, Augustin and Clarence — V.E.

Text © 2011 Catherine Austen
Illustrations © 2011 Virginie Egger

Kids Can Press acknowledges the financial support of the Government of Ontario, through the Ontario Media Development Corporation's Ontario Book Initiative; the Ontario Arts Council; the Canada Council for the Arts; and the Government of Canada, through the BPIDP, for our publishing activity.

Published in Canada by
Kids Can Press Ltd
25 Dockside Drive
Toronto, ON M5A 0B5

Published in the U.S. by
Kids Can Press Ltd.
2250 Military Road
Tonawanda, NY 14150

www.kidscanpress.com

Kids Can Press is a *Corus*™ Entertainment company

The artwork in this book was rendered in paper collage, acrylic paint and colored ink.
The text is set in Nueva.

Edited by Yvette Ghione
Designed by Karen Powers

This book is smyth sewn casebound.

Manufactured in Shen Zhen, Guang Dong, P.R. China, in 10/2010 by Printplus Limited

CM 11 0 9 8 7 6 5 4 3 2 1

Library and Archives Canada Cataloguing in Publication

Austen, Catherine, 1965–

  My cat Isis / written by Catherine Austen ; illustrated by Virginie Egger.

ISBN 978-1-55453-413-5

1. Cats—Juvenile fiction. I. Egger, Virginie, 1966– II. Title.

PS8601.U785M9 2011   jC813'.6   C2010-904762-1

My Cat Isis

WRITTEN BY Catherine Austen

ILLUSTRATED BY Virginie Egger

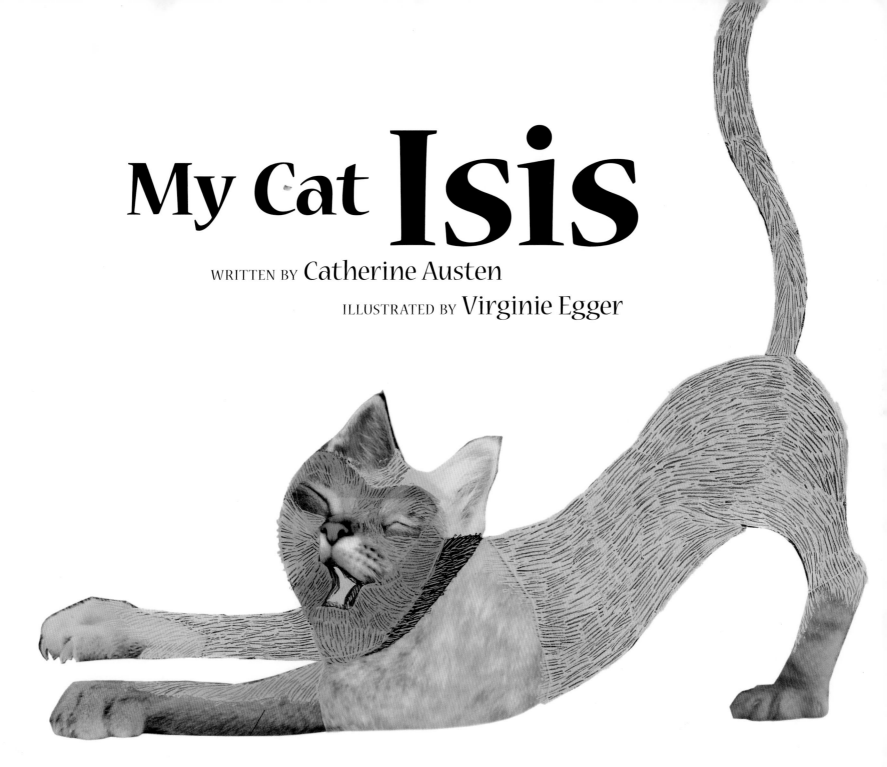

Kids Can Press

Isis was one of 1500 gods and goddesses
worshipped by the ancient Egyptians.

My Isis is the one
and only cat in our family.

Isis was the daughter of Earth and Sky.

I got my Isis when our neighbor's cat had kittens. (She was my favorite.)

Isis started off as a minor goddess, but she grew more popular with each generation.

My Isis was the runt of the litter, but with our love she grew big and strong.

Isis wore a beautiful horned headdress to show
that cattle were important in Egyptian life.

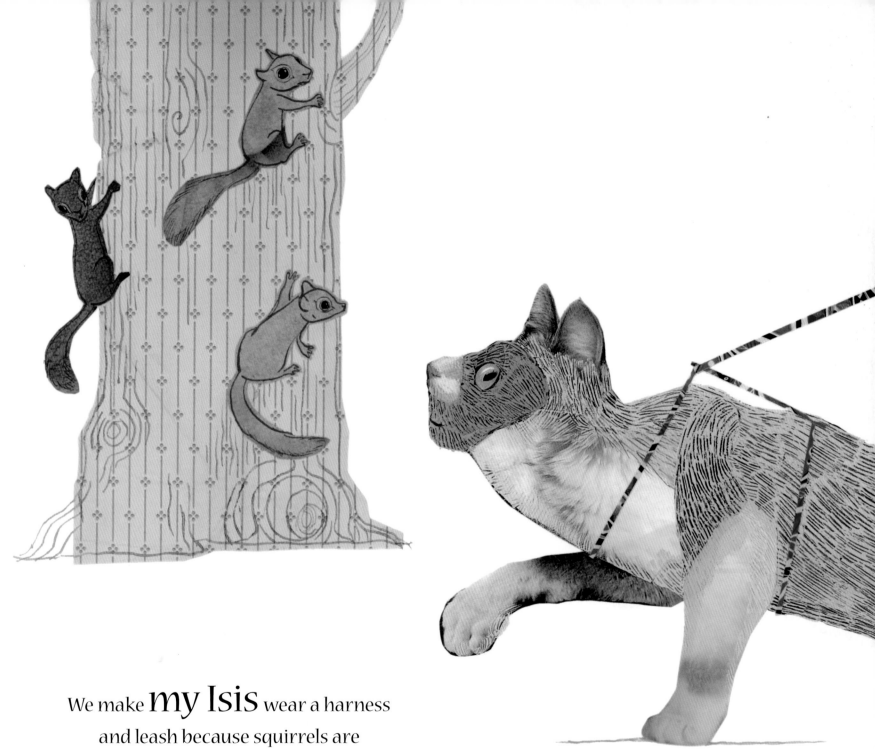

We make **my Isis** wear a harness and leash because squirrels are important in nature.

In ancient Egypt, each hour of the day and night was ruled by a different god or goddess. Isis ruled over two o'clock in the afternoon.

My Isis is usually sleeping at two o'clock in the afternoon.

Isis stood guard over the living and the dead like a devoted mother.

My Isis stands by the bird feeder and protects the seeds.

Worshippers brought Isis gifts of food, flowers
and trinkets to her many temples.

We've given **my Isis** catnip toys, rubber balls and a wind-up mouse.
(But she likes to play with the dog's tail best.)

Isis had a sister, Nephthys, and two brothers, Osiris and Seth.

My Isis has brothers and sisters in the neighborhood.

Isis and Osiris gave people agriculture, law and civilization.

My **Isis** is not very ambitious.

Isis married Osiris, but Seth tricked and killed him and stole his kingdom.

My Isis pays no attention to boy cats.

Isis was wise and talented in the ways of magic, so she was able to bring Osiris back to life.

My Isis is clever, too.
She figured out how to open
the cupboard where we
keep her kibble.

Isis and Osiris had a baby who became the sky god, Horus.

We had **my Isis** spayed.

At the height of her popularity, Isis was adored as the supreme protector of the ancient world.

My Isis bosses everyone
around, especially the dog.

The ancient Egyptians worshipped
Isis as their Ruler in Heaven
and Queen on Earth.

I love **my Isis** because
she is my cat.